The Lunchbox

A humorous
rhyming story

First published in 2006 by
Franklin Watts
338 Euston Road
London
NW1 3BH

Franklin Watts Australia
Hachette Children's Books
Level 17/207 Kent Street
Sydney
NSW 2000

A CIP catalogue record for this book is available
from the British Library.

ISBN 0 7496 6560 2 (hbk)
ISBN 0 7496 6572 6 (pbk)

Series Editor: Jackie Hamley
Series Advisors: Dr Barrie Wade, Dr Hilary Minns
Design: Peter Scoulding

Printed in China

For Tom and Ian – J.C.

The Lunchbox

Written and illustrated by
Jane Cope

W
FRANKLIN WATTS
LONDON•SYDNEY

Jane Cope

"My son, Tom, was the inspiration for this story – I made an awful lot of packed lunches for him that never got eaten! I often illustrate other people's stories, but it was great fun to do all the words and pictures myself. I really loved drawing Aunt Peg because she's so big and colourful."

Monday morning was always a rush.

"Yuck!" shouted Mum

as she washed out the mush

from last Friday's lunchbox.

"Now listen, George, please.

What's it to be, ham salad or cheese?"

"Neither," said George.

"That cheese makes me sick.

And you always make sandwiches horrid and thick!

"I'm fed up with taking that lunchbox to school! Why can't you buy me a new one that's cool?"

"WELL, I'M FED UP WITH YOUR LUNCHES!" said Mum.

"School dinner's the answer."

George looked very glum.

"Now you know until Friday
I'm working away.
So Aunt Peg will be making
your lunch every day.

"Is that all right?" Mum asked,

shutting the door.

"Great!" replied George,

"I like her food more!"

On Tuesday at eight,
Mum let Aunt Peg in.
"George!" cried Aunt Peg,
"you're looking so thin!

I've bought you a lunchbox,
isn't it cool?"
"Fantastic!" said George.
"I'll take it to school!"

13

Into the lunchbox
went crisps ...

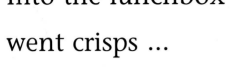

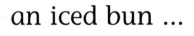

an iced bun ...

and three cans of pop.
Oh isn't food fun!

"I'll soon feed you up!"
said the smiling Aunt Peg,
as she picked off a cherry
that stuck to her leg.

On Wednesday Peg made

a huge sandwich pile:

peanut butter with chocolate –

it took quite a while!

"You see, Georgie,
food is one of the arts!"
And in case he got hungry,
she popped in six tarts.

On Thursday the lunchbox was bursting with pies.

"I made some with treacle, as a special surprise.

"And tomorrow," said Peg,
"will be our last lunch.
So I'll make sure you have
something yummy to munch!"

On Friday at lunch,

George's friends kept on gazing.

The colourful mix was just

so amazing ...

Pickled prawn twirls and
marshmallow whoppers,
blue fizzy drinks and
crackly corn poppers.

George munched,
he crunched ...

he crammed
and he slurped.

He nibbled and stuffed ...

he gulped ...

and he
burped.

23

CLANG! went the bell.

Children jumped to their feet.

And slowly George eased himself

out of his seat.

He felt hot ...

he felt cold ...

he felt rather weird.
He turned a bit green,
then just as he feared ...

25

WHOOSH! Up it all came,
the whole sugary mix.
A great rainbow fountain –
the sick of all sicks!

There were squeals and shrieks
and quite a to-do.
"Ugh! Yuck! Look, Miss,
it's all over my shoe!"

Mum picked George up early
and gave him a hug.
She wondered what caused him
to have such a bug.

"It's not fair," George thought,
"life just isn't easy
when good things are bad
and make you feel queasy."

And later on,
snuggled up cosy in bed,
George said that he might
like school dinners instead.

Notes for parents and teachers

READING CORNER has been structured to provide maximum support for new readers. The stories may be used by adults for sharing with young children. Primarily, however, the stories are designed for newly independent readers, whether they are reading these books in bed at night, or in the reading corner at school or in the library.

Starting to read alone can be a daunting prospect. READING CORNER helps by providing visual support and repeating words and phrases, while making reading enjoyable. These books will develop confidence in the new reader, and encourage a love of reading that will last a lifetime!

If you are reading this book with a child, here are a few tips:

1. Make reading fun! Choose a time to read when you and the child are relaxed and have time to share the story.

2. Encourage children to reread the story, and to retell the story in their own words, using the illustrations to remind them what has happened.

3. Give praise! Remember that small mistakes need not always be corrected.

READING CORNER covers three grades of early reading ability, with three levels at each grade. Each level has a certain number of words per story, indicated by the number of bars on the spine of the book, to allow you to choose the right book for a young reader:

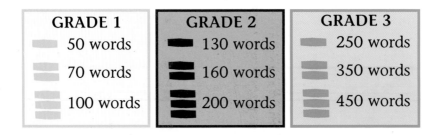

GRADE 1	GRADE 2	GRADE 3
50 words	130 words	250 words
70 words	160 words	350 words
100 words	200 words	450 words